Title: The Flea, The Green Giraffe, and Me

Just Be Publishing

D1500945

Written by Bonnie Amato & Claire Silverman

Illustrated by David Colon Delgado

ISBN-13: 978-1-7357166-2-6

Just Be Publishing Company: www.justbepublishingcompany.com

Dedication

This book was written to inspire the love of reading and creative arts for all ages.

To Kolton
Happy Reading
Claire Schuman

One day while sitting in
a tree,
I saw a Green Giraffe and
a Flea.
I knew we'd be great friends,
we three,
The Flea, the Green Giraffe,
and Me.

We rode the waves in a small sailboat.

Over the billows, we would float.

With cool, clear water as far as we could see,

for the Flea, the Green Giraffe, and Me.

Soon we landed on the shore,
and found a cave we could explore.
A buried treasure there might be,
for the Flea, the Green Giraffe, and Me.

While walking down along the beach,

We spied a mountain we could reach.

And maybe we could learn to ski.

The Flea, the Green Giraffe, and Me.

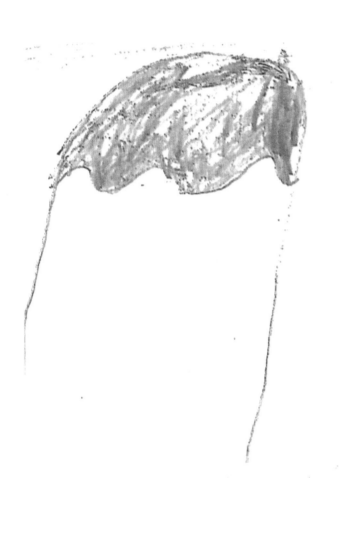

And now we're on a rocket
in the sky.
The man in the moon waves
as we go by.
The universe is so big
and free,
for the Flea, the Green Giraffe,
and Me.

Here we are at the White House gate.

We promised the president we wouldn't be late.

They're having a party at half past three,

for The Flea, the Green Giraffe, and Me.

We're headed to Hollywood, hope it's not far.

The producer said she'd make us a star.

She's putting a program on T.V.,

called, **"The Flea, The Green Giraffe, and Me."**

Now it's time to say goodbye.

I'll be brave and try not to cry.

It's been great fun,
we all agree,
the Flea, the Green Giraffe,
and Me.

Then mommy came in my room and said,
"Wake up, wake up, you sleepy head!"
But I'll always have the memory,
of the Flea, the Green Giraffe and Me.

Meet the Authors

Bonnie Amato & Claire Silverman

Bonnie has taught first and second grade as well as remedial reading over the past 35 years. She holds a B.S. in Elementary Education and a M.S. in Reading and Language Arts. She is currently a reading specialist at the CREC Reggio Magnet School of the Arts. Claire Silverman is enjoying her retirement and is a literacy volunteer in the central Connecticut area. The illustrations were created by David Colon Delgado when he was a first-grade student at the CREC Reggio Magnet School of the Arts. At time of publication he was a junior at the CREC Public Safety Academy.

Made in the USA
Middletown, DE
14 November 2020